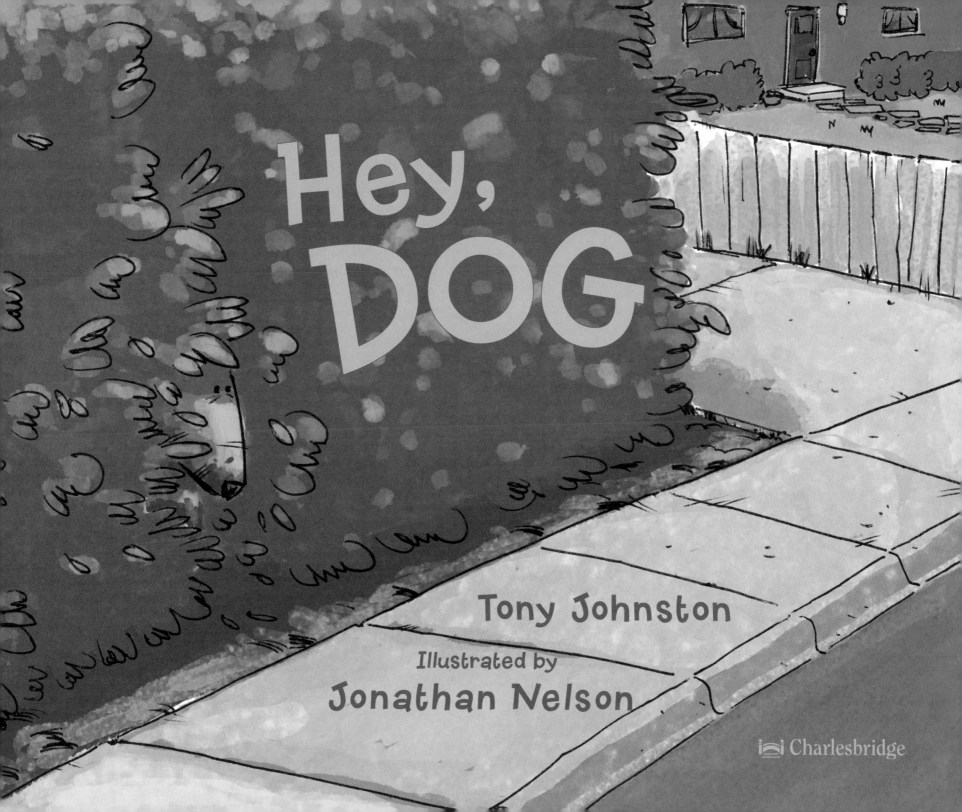

For Rachel and Chris and
their rescue dog, Winnie—T. J.

To my sisters, for acknowledging all souls,
including those with fur and whiskers—J. N.

Text copyright © 2019 by the Johnston Family Trust
Illustrations copyright © 2019 by Jonathan Nelson

Published by Charlesbridge
85 Main Street
Watertown, MA 02472
(617) 926-0329
www.charlesbridge.com

Library of Congress Cataloging-in-Publication Data
Names: Johnston, Tony, 1942- author. | Nelson, Jonathan
(Illustrator), illustrator.
Title: Hey, dog / Tony Johnston ; illustrated by Jonathan Nelson.
Description: Watertown, MA : Charlesbridge, [2019] | Summary: A boy cares
for, feeds, and helps an abused stray dog to learn to trust humans again.
Identifiers: LCCN 2018031380 (print) | LCCN 2018033760 (ebook) | ISBN
9781632897015 (ebook) | ISBN 9781632897022 (ebook pdf) | ISBN
9781580898775 (reinforced for library use)
Subjects: LCSH: Dogs—Juvenile fiction. | Dogs—Care—Juvenile fiction. |
Human-animal relationships—Juvenile fiction. | CYAC: Dogs—Fiction. |
Human-animal relationships—Fiction. | Animals—Treatment—Fiction.
Classification: LCC PZ7.J6478 (ebook) | LCC PZ7.J6478 Do 2019 (print) | DDC
[E]--dc23
LC record available at https://lccn.loc.gov/2018031380

Printed in China
(hc) 10 9 8 7 6 5 4 3 2 1

Illustrations created with blue sketch lead and graphite pencils,
    1.6 mm ballpoint pen, and Photoshop
Display type set in Family Dog Fat by Jakob Fischer
Text type set in Family Dog Regular by Jakob Fischer
Color separations by Colourscan Print Co Pte Ltd, Singapore
Printed by 1010 Printing International Limited in Huizhou,
    Guangdong, China
Production supervision by Brian G. Walker
Designed by Joyce White

The DOG is there when I walk
home from school. He's crouched in a bush.
"Hey, Dog," I say.
All bones, he runs.

"I saw a dog," I tell my mom. "He looked hungry."
"Where is he?" she asks.
"By our big tree. But he ran."

We go to see, but the dog is gone.
I leave water in my Frisbee—for
when he returns. *For when.* That's hope,
Mom would say.

That night I can't sleep.
I bet Dog's starving hungry.
And cold.

I slip out and bring him my baby quilt.
Carefully, 'cause Dog doesn't know me.
I leave him more water. And some
saved-up meatballs from my dinner.

"Hey, Dog. Hey. It's me," I whisper, soft as soft.
I want him to love my voice.
   I can't see him, but I know he's back in the bush.
In the dark I hear the leaves shiver.

Before school I tiptoe out. The meatballs are gone.
Dog's there all right.
   "Hey, Dog," I say, soft as can be.
   Nothing. He's not coming out.

Where the leaves thin, I can see he's skinny as a pin. With no tags. But he has scars. He won't look at me. He's so scared, he's shaking all over.

"Don't be afraid, Dog," I say. "It's me." Slowly I lean down and leave a hunk of my sandwich. So's not to spook him, I don't run.

After school I'm back. The sandwich is gone.
Dog's hunched in his hiding place.
"Hey, Dog. Hey. It's me."
He cringes, like I might hit him.

"Oh, Dog," I whisper, "I would never. . . ."
How could anybody do that? Tears warm my face.
I tell him, "I won't hurt you. I promise."
But he doesn't trust me. He stays put.

"Mom, I think somebody hurt Dog," I say that night.

"Why do you think that?"

"He has scars. Bad ones. And he's real flinchy. Why would somebody harm a dog? Dogs are good."

Mom looks at me with steady eyes and says fiercely, "Some people are not as good as dogs."

Dog must be lonely. So when I can,
I stop and talk to him. I give him water
and sneak him snacks.

Every time, I tell him, "I won't hurt you.
You can trust me, Dog."
      Every time, he doesn't.

"Mom," I ask. "May I feed Dog?" I don't mention
the treats I've been leaving.
    "Okay, just don't get too close. If somebody hurt him,
he might hurt back."

We buy dog food. I pay with my money.
I want Dog to be my very own—if he ever
comes out.
    At the store I fire questions:
"Is this the healthiest?"
"Is it your best?"
"Is it the most luscious?"

I dish out a Frisbee-full of dog food.
All in slow motion, I set it down, then I sit
by the bush. Mom stands close.

"Dog," I say in my pleading voice, "You have
to eat. This food is very luscious."

To show him, I pretend to taste it.

He belly-creeps from hiding, just a little bit.
Sniffing. Drooling. But he doesn't fall for the
dog-food trick.

We go, but when I glance back I grin.
Dog is wolfing that food down. I poke Mom
to show her, and she looks almost as
happy as I am.

Next day the Frisbee has been licked clean.
I sit down to talk with Dog about that.

"Good Dog," I tell him. "You have to eat all your food to grow up strong."

"You must make signs," Mom says, "to say you've found him."

"Yeah," I mumble. Deep down I've known that all along. So I write something short. I make the words as mysterious as I can— so the bad people won't find him.

"Do it over," says Mom.
"But I'm *not* sure. He's dirty."
"Do it over."

I put the found-dog signs up.
Then I hope like crazy that those bad
ones don't read it and come for him.
I hope so hard that—that night it rains.

In bed I close my eyes and imagine all my signs getting soggy, then sagging, slopping, slumping to the ground. I smile and snuggle down.

Then—"No!" I shout. Dog's getting soggy too. He might get pneumonia, even.

I grab Mom's umbrella and slurp out barefoot
through the rain and pitch the umbrella like a
tent over Dog. I go slowly, so he won't freak out.

I slop back home, sopping but happy.
Now Dog's got his very own little roof.

I go out at still-dark. The rain is gone. Stars are out, sparkling up the sky. And Dog is there, waiting for me.

For the first time I really see him. A beauty.
All wet, rumpled, scarred, and supremely muddy.
 "Hey, Dog," I say.

Slow, slow, I push my bunched fist
toward him. That's safer than offering
fingers. My heart is really beating.
I'm not breathing. Then—

Dog comes close. His fear is gone. He looks at me with soft eyes. And guess what? He licks my hand.

I can barely say a word, but at last I whisper to him.

"Hey, Dog. Come on. Let's go home."